BEAR GRYLLS

ADVENTURES

The Earthquake Challenge

BEAR GRYLLS

ADVENTURES

THE EARTHQUAKE CHALLENGE

BEAR GRYLLS
ILLUSTRATED BY EMMA McCANN

Bear Grylls

This edition published in Great Britain in 2020 by

Bear
Grylls

The Plaza, 535 Kings Road, London, SW10 0SZ

Text and illustrations copyright © Bear Grylls Ventures, 2017
Illustrations by Emma McCann
All rights reserved.

A CIP catalogue record for this book
is available from the British Library.

ISBN: 978-1-786-96017-7
Also available as an ebook

9 8

Typeset in OpenDyslexia
Printed and bound in Great Britain
by Clays Ltd, Elcograf S.p.A.

Bear Grylls is an imprint of Bonnier Books UK,
owned by Bonnier Books
Sveavägen 56, Stockholm, Sweden

www.bonnierbooks.co.uk

To the young survivor
reading this book for the first time.
May your eyes always be wide open
to adventure, and your heart full
of courage and determination to
see your dreams through.

REACH FOR THE RECORD

Fatima felt snuggly and happy in her sleeping bag, until she opened her eyes.

Then she groaned softly.

She'd woken up too soon. The tent was pitch black.

Fatima had deliberately not drunk anything after dinner. She had gone to bed a little bit thirsty, just like the night before, when she had slept soundly all through the night.

Tonight Fatima's body had other ideas.

She needed to wee.

Fatima groaned again. It was the middle of the night. But she knew she couldn't wait for morning.

She had to go.

Outside, Camp was completely silent. No voices or music from any of the other tents. The only sound she could hear was her tent-mates breathing. Chloe and Sophie were fast asleep.

Fatima hadn't told them that at home she still slept with a nightlight on. It kept the dark-monsters in her imagination away.

Fatima silently unzipped her sleeping bag. She had gone to bed in her trackies and t-shirt. She felt around for her slip-on rubber clogs, her hijab and her hoody, and put them all on. Last of all, Fatima reached for the torch under her pillow.

Then she took a deep breath, unzipped the tent flap and stood up outside.

The torch's tiny little beam wasn't much comfort. It made a circle of light on the ground so that she could see where she was going, but it didn't do much to fight the rest of the darkness.

The tent clearing was surrounded by tall trees that looked like black cut-out shapes of giant animals, stuck onto the sky. A slow wind made their branches shift and rustle as if the giant animals were muttering to each other.

"See that girl down there? We are going to get her ..."

Fatima shivered, and not just because the night wind was nippy.

It was always like this.

She *tried* to remember what the place looked like in the daylight. She had used that trick before. That way, when the light was gone and the dark closed in, she could tell herself, "There isn't really anything nasty out there."

Nothing lurking.

No giant animals.

No dark-monsters.

That was what she *tried* to tell herself. But her imagination was always a whole lot more persuasive.

5

Without realising it, Fatima had started walking a little faster. Her foot bumped against a guy rope, and she almost fell flat on her face. When she stumbled, something jogged in her hoody pocket and it took her a moment to remember what it was.

Oh yes, the compass.

Yesterday she had made a new friend, a boy called Jack. He had helped her finish the orienteering course.

She had been too afraid to go into a dark cave to stamp her clue sheet, and so he had done it for her.

He hadn't even asked why. Fatima had been very grateful for that. And he'd rescued her map from a tree hanging over the lake.

Then, for some reason, he had given her the compass.

But a compass wasn't much use now in the dark. Fatima could feel the dark-monsters creeping up behind her, but she didn't want to hurt herself, so she made herself slow down.

But that just meant the dark-monsters started creeping up more quickly. She kept her eyes facing forward.

Fatima could see the shower block's outside light on the far side of the

7

tent clearing. The closer she got
to it, the more she hurried, feeling
the dark closing in behind her.

Moths and insects buzzed around
the outside light, but that didn't
bother her. It was only the darkness
that made her feel afraid. Fatima ran
straight into the girls' bathroom.

The lights were always on inside.

She slammed the door shut behind her and puffed her cheeks out with a heavy breath while her heart slowed down. She had made it.

She put the torch down by the basins and quickly went into the toilet cubicle.

As she came out to wash her hands, she felt much better.

Then she remembered that she had to make her way back again, through the dark.

Fatima held her hands under the drier. It whirred into action for a couple of seconds. Then ...

Fzz. The electric power had died.

The drier stopped.

The lights went out.

The whole block was plunged into darkness. Even darker than outside. There was no moonlight here, no stars. Nothing to see by at all.

"Oh, come on!" she shouted.

It was a stupid power cut – the thing she hated most of all when she was at home. Fatima began to imagine the dark-monsters creeping up behind her. Her heart thudded inside her chest.

"O-okay," she said out loud. "I know there's nothing there. It's all in my mind."

She felt for where she had put the torch by the basins. Her trembling hand knocked against it and she heard it fall to the tiled floor. *Snap.* Something had definitely broken.

"No!" Fatima groaned. She knelt down and felt around for the torch. Something loose rattled inside the case when she picked it up. She flicked the switch.

And flicked it again.

Nothing. The torch was broken.

Fatima bit back a scream. There was no way out of the darkness. She was trapped in the building with her head full of dark-monsters.

2

IN THE DARK

The compass!

Fatima suddenly remembered
Jack's present. Did it have some
kind of light, maybe? Perhaps the
dial would light up like a phone?

She fumbled in her pocket. The
darkness felt alive around her, closing
in on her. Her breath was coming in

short, sharp pants. She tried to make herself breathe more slowly.

Fatima's trembling fingers closed around the compass. She yanked it out and held it in front of her eyes.

Fatima could make out the dial – just. The directions were luminous but there was no light-up face, no button to press. She couldn't use it as a torch. In fact, it was so dim that she could barely make out the directions.

Then she looked again – and for a moment it looked like there were five points on the dial, not just the usual north, south, east and west.

Strange.

Fatima gritted her teeth together, and put the compass back into her pocket.

She knew her eyes would adjust to the dark eventually. They always did. There would be tiny bits of light around the door and coming through the windows. So, eventually, she would be able to see her way out of here.

But that wasn't happening this time. *Why wasn't it happening?*

Shudders ran through Fatima's body and she forced her fears away. Okay. Okay. The room wasn't that big. She had been standing facing the sinks when the light went out.

So, all she had to do was turn
to her right and walk, and she
would reach the door.

She turned herself around, and put
her hands out in front of her. Then
she summoned up every scrap of
courage and started to walk into
the dark.

All that her hands touched was
air, and then more air. She kept
shuffling along. And then further
still. But there was no wall, no
door. Was the room bigger than
she remembered?

Then, thank goodness, she could
see a glimmer of light. The black
was turning slowly into grey. She
could make out shapes.

But the shapes weren't familiar. Fatima winced as she tried to match the shapes with her memories of the bathroom in daylight.

In the far distance, Fatima thought she heard a rumble. Was it a thunderstorm? It was a long way away and it was more like she *felt* it than heard it.

Then, out of the darkness, her hands touched something strange, something soft. Fatima gasped in shock and pulled her hand away.

Whatever it was, it wasn't the wall.

It felt like *clothes*. Clothes hanging on a rack.

Weird.

Then Fatima thought she saw someone standing, a few metres to the side of her. They weren't moving.

Fatima realised it was too thin and too still to be a person.

It was a shop dummy. And there was another one behind it.

Then she made out racks of clothes all around her.

"What?" Fatima exclaimed. "Where ...? How ...?"

Fatima realised that she was no longer in the girls' bathroom at Camp.

Somehow she was in a clothes store. A dark, deserted clothes store. Her mind spun. It was impossible.

Had she sleepwalked? She had heard of people doing that. But if she had somehow sleepwalked from Camp into the nearest town then she had gone a very long way.

But it didn't matter how, she told herself. She still had the same problem – she had to find a way out. And she only ever came up with the same solution – keep going until you reach a wall or a door.

Fatima began to walk again.

Then she heard that rumble again. Louder, closer. It was like a train, or the main road near where she lived. The sound ran from the floor and up her legs before it reached her ears.

But then other noises started to add to it. Weird creaks and groans that she felt in her teeth and her stomach. Fatima could feel herself starting to panic again. Her legs were trembling.

Then Fatima realised it wasn't fear

that made her legs do that. It was the
floor. The ground really was shaking.

One of the clothes racks began
to slide across the floor.

Then there was a cre-e-e-a-a-k
and suddenly part of the roof fell
in. It smashed into the floor on the
other side of the room.

Fatima didn't usually scream, even
when she was frightened, but she
screamed loudly now.

And then there was another cre-
e-e-a-a-k ... right above her. Fatima
broke into a run and the shaking
floor threw her from side to side.
She yelled and stumbled, waving
her arms about to keep upright.

A door flew open in the distance.

At last, a rectangle of daylight!
She could just about make out a man
standing outlined in the doorway. But
Fatima didn't feel scared. Instead, she
felt relief. She wasn't alone, after all.

The man spun round and spotted
her.

"Take cover!" he called over to her
urgently. "You need to get down on
the floor, quick as you can!"

Fatima ignored him. She just wanted
to get out. She started to run towards
the daylight, but then the floor gave
an extra hard shake and Fatima's feet
disappeared from beneath her.

3

AFTERSHOCK

Fatima landed on the hard ground
with a thump that knocked the breath
out of her. She gasped. The floor was
still shaking, and she could hear the
ceiling creaking above her.

The man who had been trying to
help her dropped to all fours.

"Over here!" he called, as he jerked

his thumb at a table that was covered with scarves. "Quick! Follow me, and stay low!"

He showed the way by crawling over to the table. Fatima followed him. The man helped Fatima get beneath the table, to protect her from the dust and debris that was falling from above.

"Try to keep hold of the table leg," the man shouted over the din. "It will stop the table shaking away from us."

Fatima grabbed hold of the table leg he pointed at while he took hold of another one.

"What's happening?" Fatima gasped.

"It's the aftershock from an earthquake," he said, fixing her with a stare that said he knew what he was doing. "And when that happens, the first two things to do are get down, and, if you're indoors, find shelter that won't fall in on you."

She could see him clearly now in the light coming through the open door. He was tall, with dark hair and a tanned face.

"Will it all fall down?" Fatima asked nervously.

"It shouldn't. They build modern buildings to stay up in an earthquake – but that doesn't stop everything inside being thrown about."

A few seconds later, the shaking died away. The noise that sounded like a runaway train went off into the distance.

"That's probably it for the moment," said the man. "Let's get out of here."

Getting out suited Fatima just fine, despite what he had said about modern buildings not falling down. She had felt this one shaking like jelly and she didn't trust it.

They climbed quickly out from under the table. Clothes racks had been shaken out of place by the quake, and just inside the door there was a cleaner's trolley lying on its side with the brooms and buckets all tumbled out.

"So, are you Suki or Anika?" the man asked. "And where are the others?"

Fatima blinked in surprise.

"Um – I'm on my own. I'm Fatima."

"Oh." It looked like it was the man's turn to be surprised.

"Okay, well, nice to meet you, Fatima. I'm Bear and I'm here to help guide you out of here." He paused. "This isn't going to be an easy journey."

He looked around, then back at her with a smile. "Are you ready for an adventure?"

Fatima looked around at the remains of the store.

"As long as we can have the adventure outside," she told him.

Bear grinned.

"Trust me, getting outside is a priority."

Together, they started to move towards the nearest door and the light. But when they stepped out, Fatima was surprised. She had thought they would be exiting the building into the outdoors.

Instead, she saw that they were in an indoor shopping mall with stores all around on multiple levels.

There had been a glass roof
above, but it had shattered in
the earthquake. Piles of glass
lay all around them on the floor.

She looked up through the open
roof above and could see daylight
flooding in.

The damage from the quake was everywhere. An ice-cream stall lay on its side. All the tables and chairs at an outdoor restaurant were jumbled all over the place.

"The earthquake hit the city badly," said Bear. "It's been evacuated so everyone has left."

"So what are you doing here?" Fatima asked.

"I came to find —" he began, but then he stopped. He cocked his head like he was listening for something. "Can you hear that?" Bear asked.

Fatima strained her ears. She wasn't sure what she was listening for.

So it came as a surprise when
Bear put his hands to his mouth
and bellowed: "HELLO!"

This time Fatima heard what he
heard. It sounded like a small kid
shouting back.

"Help!"

"It was that way," Fatima said.
She pointed across the mall. Bear
started walking, and once again
he shouted: "HELLO!"

There was another cry. This time
they could both immediately tell
where it was.

"It's from in here." Bear hurried
over towards a large recycling bin

on wheels that lay on its side against a wall where it had been thrown by the quake. He thumped a hand on it, and someone inside shouted back.

Fatima gasped with horror. She couldn't imagine being trapped in one of those. It would be so dark. And how could they breathe in there?

They had to get whoever was in there out, as fast as they could.

Bear tried to lift the skip up, heaving with all his strength. But he couldn't move it, and the lid was wedged closed.

"The lid must have got bent when it toppled over. I need something to lever it with ..." Bear muttered as he looked around.

"How about this?" Fatima asked.

Some of the tables had parasols, all furled up, and she picked one up. It was longer than she was, and she staggered a little with it until Bear took it from her.

"Smart!" he declared with a smile. "Good work."

He rammed the tip of the parasol into the crack between the lid and the rest of the skip, and strained. The lid suddenly flew open. Fatima and Bear peered in.

Two small girls and a little boy peered back, blinking in the sudden light.

4

DROP – COVER – HOLD ON

"Hi," Bear said with a friendly smile.
"You're Anika, Suki and Ryan, right?
I'm Bear. I promised your mum I'd
come and get you. She recorded
this for you."

He held up a phone. The screen
showed a woman waving.

"Hi, kids. This is my friend Bear,"

she said. "I twisted my ankle so I can't come for you, but I'm okay. Bear said he will make sure you get to me safely. You can trust him."

"Can I talk to Mummy?" the little boy asked.

"You're Ryan, right? Not right now, little buddy. Mummy recorded that earlier. There's no signal to talk to her now."

Ryan's face started to crumple. Bear quickly hoisted him out of the skip and spun him round before putting him down, which distracted him and made him laugh.

"Don't worry, buddy. I know where Mummy is," Bear promised.

"I'm Anika," said the biggest girl as she climbed out. She was a bit younger than Fatima. "We waited like Mummy said, and she told us to make sure we were under cover, so when the roof started to fall in, I made us all hide in here and I closed the lid."

"Well, that was a very wise move," Bear agreed. "But if you ever have to hide in something like this again, try to prop the lid open a little bit so you can get out again."

He lifted the smaller girl out of the skip.

"So, you must be Suki," he said to her. "And this is my friend Fatima, who's going to help me get you all home safely."

Fatima smiled and nodded. She was used to helping out with her little brothers and sisters.

"Sure," she said, and Bear flashed her a grateful smile.

Then Bear gathered them all together and knelt down beside them.

"Now listen carefully, team. We are going to need to work smart and work together, if we're going to get home in one piece."

He paused, and looked at each of them in turn. "But it won't be easy and we will face many challenges. Do you think you are able to be strong and brave enough to make it?"

They all nodded and Ryan and Suki
jumped up and down shouting: "Easy-
peasy!"

"Then let's do this!"

"Okay," Bear said, "first up, we're
in the middle of a badly damaged city.
We can't trust any building to stay
upright. There's no clean water to
drink, or electricity to keep us warm
and give us light. We're on our own."

Their smiles and enthusiasm rapidly
turned into worried looks.

"But our priorities are just the
same as if we were out in the wild
somewhere – protection, rescue,
water and food."

The kids were all ears as Bear went on.

"Like I've told Fatima, there may be more aftershocks. If that happens, the rules are drop, cover and hold on. Drop, so you don't hurt yourself by falling."

Bear dropped quickly to the ground to demonstrate, and the kids laughed.

He got back up and dusted himself
down with a smile.

"Cover means get under something
that will protect you from falling
stuff. Maybe a table – or a big bin!"

Anika laughed.

"And *hold on* means just that,"
Bear continued. "Your shelter will
be shaking around just like you,
so you need to keep it with you –
like we did with the table, Fatima."

He looked around at them all.

"Now, our first job is to get
everything we need together.

And as we're in a shopping mall that shouldn't be hard. We'll start over there."

Bear pointed to a sports store, but frowned when he glanced down at their feet.

The store was on the far side of a sea of broken glass. Fatima was only wearing rubber clogs, with open backs, and the kids had sandals. Bear was wearing leather boots that were scuffed but which looked tough.

That meant that only he could walk across all the glass safely.

"I could carry you, I suppose ..." he thought out loud.

"Hang on," Fatima said. "I know just the thing!"

She ducked quickly back into the clothes store behind them. What she needed was right by the door, in the light. There was the cleaner's trolley – and a broom with a nice wide head. Bear smiled when he saw it.

"Perfect! Okay, everyone, follow me and walk exactly where I walk."

And so they all walked across the mall in single file, with Bear pushing the broom in front to brush the broken glass aside.

Fatima had never thought that just walking across a mall could be an adventure. The city had been built to be a safe place for humans. The quake had turned it against them.

At first, Fatima hung back at the entrance to the sports store. It was dark and she would rather stay in the daylight.

But the sports store had bigger windows than the clothes store, so it wasn't quite as dark inside. And they could see even better when Bear found some torches and batteries.

Finding boots for them all took a while because none of the younger kids knew their shoe sizes. Fatima had to help them by guessing what their sizes were, and then picking out the labels on the shoeboxes with the torch.

Bear made sure they all chose boots made of tough leather with good solid grips underneath. He also picked out some fleeces, light waterproof jackets and hats for everyone, and gave them each a backpack and a tough plastic sports bottle each.

The kids all looked like it was their birthday as they proudly wore their brand-new stuff. Bear added some cooking gear – pans and plates – to his own backpack.

Bear added up the cost of everything they had taken, and left some banknotes tucked under the till to pay for it all.

"Always be honest. Just because we are in an emergency doesn't mean we lose our morals," he explained. "We do what is right. Always. Now, let's find an exit."

Fatima studied a map of the shopping mall outside the sports store. The mall was shaped like a big cross, and they were down one of the arms.

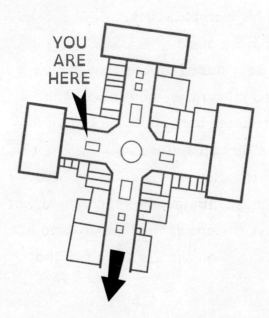

YOU
ARE
HERE

"The nearest exit's this way," Fatima said, pointing at the end of the next arm.

She remembered Bear's list of priorities for a survivor. *Protection, rescue, water, food.*

"And there's a supermarket on the way, so we can get supplies there."

"Good girl, Fatima." Bear looked proudly at her. "Just like being in the wild – you need to plan your way ahead as much as you can."

They all walked down to the centre of the mall. Anika and Suki held hands. Fatima held Ryan's hand, not just to comfort him but to stop him slipping on the broken glass that was everywhere. She felt the glass crunch beneath their feet and was extra grateful for the tough footwear.

The little group turned right towards the exit – and Fatima stopped in dismay.

"Oh."

Most of the mall had been left standing by the quake – but not this bit. At the far end there was just a pile of rubble.

And there was no sign of a way out.

5

EXIT STRATEGY

"Oh no!" Suki burst into tears. Anika was putting on a brave face. Ryan hadn't quite worked out what this meant.

"It's okay," Fatima said quickly. "There must be another way out. Right, Bear?"

"In a big place like this? There's

bound to be," Bear agreed with a smile to show the kids he wasn't worried. "But first things first. Let's stock up on supplies. Fatima, bring the team and help me."

The supermarket was the last shop before the enormous pile of rubble.

Fatima gulped and swallowed as they all stood in the entrance. The lines of shelves disappeared into the darkness. She could imagine dark-monsters all lurking at the back, just out of sight.

Bear flashed his torch about, making crazy shadows jump around. Cans, bottles and boxes all lay about on the floor.

When he ran the beam over the
ceiling, Fatima could see pipes and
metal bars through square black holes
where roof tiles had fallen down.
Some of the ceiling lights had come
loose and dangled from their cables.

Fatima did *not* want to go into the
darkness and the shadows. But she
had to be brave, for the kids' sake.
Bear had asked her to help him.

They moved slowly into the store.
There were lines of abandoned
trolleys and baskets at the tills,
all full of shopping. When the quake
had hit, people must have just left
their trolleys and run.

Bear picked through the things
in the nearest one.

"Milk – already gone off. Frozen pizza – also gone off, and we couldn't cook it easily on a campfire anyway. Soft drinks – let's pass on that. They just make you thirstier than when you began. We'll do our own shopping."

"Anika and Suki, and Fatima and Ryan – you each get an empty trolley of your own. Stick together in pairs. I'll keep this one."

"*Three* trolleys?" said Suki.

"That's a lot of shopping," Anika added.

"They're not all for shopping," Bear said. Fatima remembered his talk about the earthquake drill, and she immediately guessed what he meant.

"If there's a shock while we're in the store," she said, "we turn our trolleys upside down and hide under them."

Bear smiled and nodded.

"You've got it. There may be more stuff falling from the ceiling, or tins dropping off shelves," he said. "You'll be safer inside a metal cage. Okay, team, let's do this."

They moved through the store in
single file with their three trolleys.
Fatima let Ryan sit in the baby seat
on hers. Their torches lit the way
down the aisles and light reflected
back off the shelves.

Fatima could imagine dark-monsters
in the aisles on either side, pacing
along to keep track of the little
group.

Bear picked up some packets
of energy bars, and lots of tins
of tuna and baked beans.

"Small, easy to carry and you can eat them hot or cold," he said cheerfully. "Also they'll pack in the energy when we eat them, and they're something to look forward to. Let's get something to wash it down with."

In the drinks section he found several large bottles of still spring water.

"Okay," Bear said, "let's see your nice new sports bottles, shall we?"

He lined their bottles up in his trolley, and began to pour the bottled water into them.

"Mummy says bottled water is a rip-off," said Suki.

"Well, it can be," Bear agreed as the water glugged into Fatima's bottle. "It's a luxury, really, because it costs about three hundred times more to take it out of the ground and put it in a plastic bottle than it does to just drink it out of the tap."

He smiled at them. "But, here and now, we can't trust what's in the taps. The quake could have cracked pipes open and it could all be mixed up with sewage. So bottled water is safer."

Ryan tugged at Fatima's sleeve.

"What's sewage?" he asked.

"It's what goes down the toilet," she told him.

"Yuck!"

Fatima smiled — not just at Ryan's reaction but because now they would be heading out into the daylight again. It was so dark and her heart was beating so fast in here. She couldn't wait to get outside.

So when Bear walked further into the supermarket, her heart sank. He flashed his torch over the signs on the ceiling.

"One more thing ..."

Bear had found the pharmacy section. He took a couple of packets of bandages off the shelves, and rummaged through the other bottles and boxes.

"Got it!" Bear sounded pleased with something he had found. He held up a small bottle. "Potassium permanganate. Very useful for disinfecting cuts, purifying water ..."

Bear was on a roll now, grabbing things off the shelf as fast as he could. "And also let's get some tape and some blister plasters. Just in case. Okay, let's go."

They wheeled their trolleys back to the entrance, where Bear again left some money for everything they had taken.

Fatima sighed deeply with relief to be back outside in the daylight.

Finally! No more hanging around in that dark place!

Bear unpacked his trolley into everyone's backpacks. He distributed it all according to how big they were, so that he ended up carrying the most and Ryan had his water bottle and a single can, which he was very proud of.

"And now let's find our way out of here!"

They headed back to the map of the mall and crowded around it. Bear pointed with a broken pen that he had spotted lying on the floor, and showed the group where they were on the diagram.

Then he traced the way to the blocked exit.

YOU
ARE
HERE

"So we can't go that way. Which means ..."

He frowned as he moved his pen back and forward across the map, searching for another route out. But there were no other exits marked.

It seemed that there was only one way in or out of the mall, and that way was blocked by a hundred tons of rubble.

6

ROOFTOP VIEW

All the children turned and looked up at Bear questioningly.

Fatima knew this wasn't looking good.

"Could we shift the pile? Bit by bit?" she asked. "I mean, we could put the bricks in the trolleys and wheel them away?"

"I'm just a bit wary of disturbing it," Bear told her. "You don't know what else might then come crashing down. Let's try to find another way. All these shops must have fire exits." He jerked a thumb back at the supermarket.

The kids seemed okay with that but Fatima felt it like a thump in her stomach.

There was nothing wrong with Bear's plan ... except for one thing.

Go back into that big, dark, empty place? We just got out of there!

Bear seemed to notice something. He took her gently to one side.

"You okay, Fatima?" he asked in a quiet voice.

Fatima wanted to say "I'm fine", because that was what she always did. She had never admitted it to anyone but her parents – but no one had ever needed her help like Bear did.

He deserved to know the truth.

Saying it out loud felt like the bravest thing she had ever done.

"I'm really afraid of the dark," she whispered.

Fatima braced herself to hear all the usual stuff like: "stop being silly", "there's nothing to to be scared of" and "that's childish".

But Bear surprised her.

"I can understand that," he
murmured. "I expect you've heard
it all before, right?" he asked.
"You've no doubt told yourself
it's all in your head, it's not real ..."

Fatima nodded.

"It doesn't help," she said.

"Well, admitting there's a problem
is always the first step to fixing
anything. And you've done that,
which is such a big step for you.
But, you see ..."

Bear tapped his head with a finger.

"The victory starts in the same place as the fear. Up here. Your brain is amazing and it's there to help you. You just need to start learning how to get your thoughts and emotions to work for you rather than against you."

"I can't, and they don't." Fatima still couldn't speak louder than a whisper.

She looked at the dark entrance
to the supermarket. "I just know
that I can't walk all the way through
that place again."

He went on. "You don't have to do
it all at once. But you do have to stop
expecting a negative response. Stop
feeding the fear. You can do this and
your brain can help you," Bear told
her.

"You are going to tell yourself
that it is an irrational fear and that

you are not going to let that fear
dictate how you live. Okay?"

"Okay. Sort of. But how do I do
that?"

"Well, firstly, know that the fear
isn't based on truth and then make
a decision to walk towards it."

Bear paused to let his advice sink
in. Then he continued.

"Together, we will take one positive
step towards the fear, towards the
dark. We will do it with courage, and
when we feel the fear rising we are
going to tell it to back away, and then
we are going to keep going."

He smiled as he saw a mix of

excitement and trepidation building
in Fatima's eyes.

"And then once we have done that,
then we do it again. And again. Until
the fear goes away and your control
of the situation grows. Because all
those positive steps will add up."

Bear looked right at her. "Can
you do it?"

Fatima looked at the floor and
then up at him – and she nodded.

"Good for you, Fatima. This is how
you are going to conquer your fear."
He paused. "I can't do it for you. But
you can do it."

Fatima smiled nervously.

They went back into the supermarket.
There were grumbles from the girls.
Only Ryan seemed happy because he
could flash his torch about.

At first it wasn't so bad. They had
been here before. But this time they
pressed on through, all the way to
the back.

Bear led them through a door and it
was like going into a dark maze. Store
rooms, offices and more corridors.
Fatima hadn't realised there were
so many rooms in a supermarket.

Her heart thudded inside her so
strongly. She wanted to run away
as fast as she could, but she forced

herself to keep walking. She held
on to Ryan's hand and kept going.
One foot in front of the other, just
like Bear had said.

Fatima kept telling herself that
the fear had no power over her,
and that by moving forward and
kicking the fear away each time
it rose up, then she could do this.

And it was actually working.

Eventually they came to a solid
door with a metal bar across it and
the words FIRE EXIT printed above
it in red letters. Fatima imagined
all the lovely sunshine on the other
side and felt relief wash over her.

"Okay, here goes!"

Bear pushed on the bar and the door swung open ... into a dark concrete passage. Fatima's heart plummeted.

Bear's torch beam played over a pile of rubble further along, where the ceiling had fallen in.

But then his torch lit up a flight of metal stairs at the end of the passage.

"I'll bet those take us all the way up to the roof – and up there, chances are good there'll be a metal ladder or a fire escape down the outside of the building."

The group edged their way forward into the darkness. Ever further.

The stairs took them up a square concrete stairwell. Into the darkest place yet. They moved upwards in their bubble of torchlight.

Fatima's heart thudded inside her but she kept doing as she had done before – she just kept going.

Another solid door blocked their way at the top. Bear rammed his shoulder against it and it flew open!

The kids cheered as daylight flooded into the stairwell. Fatima breathed a sigh of pure happiness.

Bear winked at her. "I knew you could do it." He peered around. "Everyone hold hands with Fatima or me until I'm sure it's safe."

Fatima quickly realised why Bear wanted to hold the kids back.

"There's the fire escape!" Suki shouted.

Fatima had to pull Suki and Ryan back as they both suddenly tried to run across the flat roof.

A railing ran all the way around the roof. Right opposite them there was a gap, and Fatima could see the top of some metal stairs.

The staircase went all the way down to the ground – but there was a small gap between the top stair and the building. The quake had torn it away from the wall.

Bear approached it cautiously, and prodded it with his boot. It creaked and groaned and wobbled.

"Not that way," Bear decided. "Our weight could pull it off the building altogether. We'll find another way down, but while we're up here, let's take the opportunity to plan our journey. The main priority is to get out of town and meet up with your families."

Fatima looked out at the city. Quake damage was everywhere. In one direction she could see a whole bunch of tall buildings and skyscrapers. Most of the windows were broken and some office blocks had cracks running up them. That was probably the city centre.

"So –" she pointed in the opposite direction – "we want to head that way?"

Bear smiled and nodded.

"Yes. Towards the main road out of town. That's our priority. Head west. Okay, let's see how to get down."

The small group patrolled slowly around the edge of the roof.

But there were no other fire escapes. The nearest building was maybe five metres away – way too far to jump.

They were back where they had started. Fatima thought through their options.

"So the only way down is a fire escape that is too dangerous to use, or ..." She swallowed nervously. "Or go back into the building?"

Bear looked around the roof, and smiled.

"Or," he said, "we climb down!"

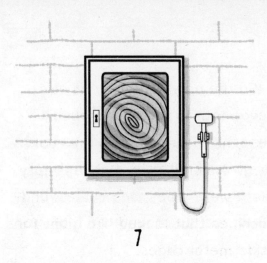

HOSE HARNESS

"Climb?" Fatima asked in surprise.

Bear surely didn't mean climb down the dangerous stairs.

She took a peek over the railing that ran around the top of the building and down the wall. It was smooth bricks. It would be impossible to find handholds on a wall like that.

And it was a long way down.

Fatima looked around the roof.
It wasn't completely flat or empty.
There were pipes, and cables, and
machines that looked like giant fans
inside metal cages.

And then she saw it.

A sign saying FIRE HOSE above a
glass case, which was fixed to the
wall next to the door where they
had come out. A hose was curled
up inside it.

Bear was already on it. He smashed
the glass with a hammer clipped to
the wall, and started to pull the hose
so that it all unreeled onto the roof.

"We're about twenty metres off the ground," he said seriously, "and it says this is twenty-five metres long. I'll make a harness and lower you one by one." He looked at Fatima.

"Fatima, I'll be holding on at this end, and I'm going to need someone to look after the kids on the ground, so are you okay to go first?"

"Um – sure," Fatima said. "But I'm heavier than them," she added. "Can you hold my weight?"

"I won't be holding anyone's weight. I have a plan. Don't worry!"

By now all of the hose was uncoiled on the roof. Bear dragged it all over to the railing and looped one end of

the hose around it. Then he looped
it around once more.

"The railing will be like a pulley
that takes your weight, and then I
just have to hold the hose and let
you down gently," he said. "Taking
a double wrap around it means it
will be easier for me to lower you."

Bear started to tie a loop in the
hose at the other end.

"Classic bowline knot," Bear said.
"Make a loop, then the end is like a
rabbit coming out of the hole, round
the tree and back down the hole!"

As he spoke he threaded the hose
in the way he described, with the end
of the hose acting as the rabbit.

Fatima perked up. "I remember learning that knot in Scouts!"

"Nice! Well, now's the time to test it! Put your arms through here, so it's under your armpits, and then lower your arms to your side to trap the hose."

Fatima did as Bear instructed.

"Keep your armpits clamped to your side," he added, as he tightened the bowline around her. "Now hold the hose in front of you and don't let go."

Bear looked Fatima in the eyes. "You ready for this?"

"Ready!" she said with newfound confidence.

Butterflies still fluttered
in Fatima's stomach as
she climbed backwards
over the railing and hung
over the four-storey
drop, but she knew she
had conquered her fears
before and she knew she
could do it again.

"Don't look down," Bear
said. "Just keep your eyes
on the wall in front of you
and your armpits tight.
Push your legs out against
the wall so you aren't
hanging just on the hose.
Ready? Here goes."

The wall began to move
slowly past Fatima's eyes.

It was a smooth, steady ride down
to the ground, as she slowly walked
backwards down the sheer face of the
wall. The hose ran smoothly over the
railing and Bear could take her weight
with no problem.

In no time at all Fatima felt her
boots touch the ground.

She wriggled out of the harness
and stood back so that Bear could
pull it back up. While he was doing
that, Fatima looked around.

The city felt eerie with no one
else about. Cities were meant to be
full of noise. Usually there were cars
and people, alarms and trains, and
aeroplanes overhead. Noise was just
there, even if your brain tuned it out.

You only really noticed it when it wasn't there any more. Every movement she made, even her breathing, seemed to echo. It was weird, but it wasn't frightening – in the daylight.

But Fatima gulped as she thought ahead.

She didn't know what time it was but she could see it was past midday. The sun was starting its journey down towards the horizon, and she guessed they would still be in the city as night fell. They would have to find somewhere to sleep.

It would be silent, and it would be *dark*.

No! she told herself firmly. *Don't think like that.*

She would cross that bridge when she came to it. She would conquer her fear, again and again, until it lost all its grip on her, like Bear had said.

She smiled to herself. She was sounding like a survivor.

Suki came down next, with her eyes squeezed tight shut. She even kept them closed while Fatima helped her out of the harness, until she could actually believe she was on solid ground.

Then came Ryan, then Anika, and last of all Bear himself. He looped the hose over him, just like the others had, but he held the end that was wrapped twice around the railings in his hands. Then he slowly started to lower himself down the wall.

"Great work, team!" Bear smiled at them as he touched the ground. "Right, let's find an open space, away from anything that might decide to fall on us, and then I think we've all earned a quick drink before we push on."

They walked towards the shopping mall's car park. It was wonderful to finally have the big dark building behind them.

But after only a few metres, Fatima heard a noise like an approaching train.

She had heard it before ...

"It's another aftershock!" Bear called.

In another half second the ground began to tremble.

Bear dropped down to all fours. "Everyone, down on the ground!"

$KMnO_4$

8

CAR CAMP

Drop – cover – hold on! That was what Bear had told them before.

Fatima pulled Ryan down to join her on the ground as bits fell off the mall building with loud crashes.

But *drop* was all they could do. The only *cover* was the abandoned cars on the other side of the car park,

too far away to run to. And there
was nothing to *hold on* to at all.

"Curl up!" Bear called. "Protect
your head and neck with your hands,
like this."

He curled into the tightest ball he
could, with his hands over his head.
Then he uncurled and made sure
the girls were doing it, while Fatima
looked after Ryan.

Glass shattered and metal crunched
as the shock rocked the abandoned
cars. The tarmac felt gritty and
sticky, and it stank of petrol and oil.

Fatima could hear everything
creaking and groaning. She felt like
a bug curled up on the pavement that

could be squished at any moment.

But the rumbling died away and
Fatima uncurled slowly. There were
fresh cracks in the walls of the mall
building, and a haze of dust and dirt
in the air.

But everything was now still again.

They gathered themselves together
and moved off as a group.

No one spoke much and there was
tension in the air.

They knew an aftershock could hit
again at any time.

Bear tried to lighten the mood
and insisted they all had a picnic

together, sat on a bench at a bus stop. Everyone snacked on an energy bar and washed it down with water.

It was a hot, sunny day, and Fatima had made sure everyone wore their new hats from the sports store to protect their heads and necks from the heat.

Bear isn't the only one who knows how to survive, she thought to herself with a smile.

Then they started to walk.

The little group hiked for a couple of hours. Suki and Ryan took turns riding on Bear's shoulders. They kept to the middle of the road, in case buildings started falling.

Soon they were out of the town centre. They walked past a deserted train station and a big industrial estate. Eventually they came to houses, where people had lived. All of them were abandoned and empty now.

Meanwhile Fatima kept an eye on the sun. It was getting lower and the shadows were getting longer. The sunlight that hit the tops of buildings was turning red.

She swallowed nervously. It was definitely sunset. Her precious daylight was running out.

"Are we nearly there yet?" Anika asked tiredly. Bear smiled gently and told her what Fatima had already guessed.

"We're going to have to camp out tonight, but we should be back with your mum before lunch tomorrow. She's in a temporary hospital where they are fixing her foot, but she'll feel a whole lot better the moment she sees you all."

Bear called a halt when they reached a small park with a children's playground, surrounded by shops and houses.

Next to it were two cars that must have once been neatly parked on the street.

Now they were both turned upside down, having been thrown around like toys by the earthquake.

"We can't drive these damaged cars but they are perfect shelters," Bear said. "The steel shells will protect us, and keep the weather and scavengers out."

"What's a scavenger?" Suki asked.

"It's an animal," Anika told her.

"Kind of," Bear agreed. "It's any animal looking for free food. Dogs, cats, urban foxes – they'll all be used to humans feeding them. Now the humans have gone, they'll be looking for food on their own – and they won't all be friendly."

While the kids played on the swings, Bear and Fatima checked the cars for leaking oil and petrol – anything that could catch fire or be unsafe.

"You and the kids can sleep in one," Bear suggested to Fatima. "And I can take this other one."

The roofs inside both cars were big flat surfaces that would work fine as beds to lie on. But they would need something to protect themselves from the cold ground below.

"Cut up the seats, and get the foam out of them," Bear said to Fatima. "You can use it as insulation tonight, to stop the ground sucking all the warmth away. I'll make us a fire."

Trusted with a knife! Fatima thought with a smile. Her mum would have a fit. But she knew Bear well enough by now to understand that if he trusted her to be smart with a task then she would live up to the challenge.

She took the knife and got to work.

By the time she had finished Bear had collected some dead branches from the bushes in the park. Then he got some bandages out of his backpack and made a small pile on a paving slab.

Next he took out the bottle of potassium permanganate he had found in the supermarket, and poured some into the bandages.

Last of all he took a bottle of antifreeze that he had found in the boot of one of the cars, and poured it over the pile.

He waited a few seconds ...

Whoomph! The whole pile of bandages caught fire.

They all whooped with delight at the fire in front of them.

Bear grinned.

"That's potassium permanganate reacting with glycerin in the antifreeze – my favourite chemical reaction! Pretty cool, eh? But to keep it burning, we need fuel."

He started to put the dead branches on top of the fire, one by one, and they began to burn too.

They sat on some cushions that Bear had found in the back of one of the cars, with travel rugs wrapped around them. Bear heated baked beans and tuna in a metal saucepan over the flames, and then dealt out their helpings onto plastic plates.

Fatima hadn't realised how hungry she was until she started to wolf it all down with a plastic fork. The day's adventures had really taken it out of her.

By now the sun had gone completely down. Darkness rushed in over the city, right up to their tiny circle of firelight. Shadows closed in and peered over their shoulders.

Fatima turned her back on them and made herself focus on the fire, and on her friends. She had light and she had company.

Bear was eating with the rest of them but he kept looking around for scavengers. And that was why Bear was the first one to see the light.

"Look," he said. "Over there."

Some distance away there was a single beam of light shining up into the sky.

"What is it?" Fatima asked.

"It could be a signal," Bear said. "Maybe there's someone trapped there – someone who needs help." He pulled a face. "I have to go and see who it is. Fatima, I'll have to leave you here, in charge."

"Me?" Fatima said in alarm. She had just begun feeling safe and secure, but suddenly all that vanished.

Bear smiled and lowered his voice so that only she could hear.

"Keep stepping up to the challenge, Fatima," he said. "You've got this. You are doing so well. But someone else needs help and I should go ..."

"Um. I guess." Fatima swallowed, but she nodded.

She was going to be on her own, with three small children to care for, and no Bear, and darkness all around her.

9

FATIMA IN CHARGE

Fatima wanted to call out, "Come back!" as Bear disappeared into the darkness.

But Bear had told her she could manage, and the children already looked a little bit frightened. She didn't want to let Bear or the kids down. Bear had believed in her before and she had proved she could do it ...

No. There was no way she would let them down by giving up.

"Okay," Fatima said instead. "Who knows any songs?"

And so they taught each other different songs that they knew. It made a happy sound and it pushed the dark back a little bit.

Bear had cut a small pile of sticks, and whenever the fire went down Fatima put another one on the flames. The fire picked up again and the darkness stayed back.

Then something moved at the edge of the light. Fatima gasped as two yellow eyes stared at her.

But half a second later, the owner
of the eyes came into view. It was
a black-and-white cat. The three
children were immediately all over
it. It purred loudly and seemed
especially interested in Ryan's
leftover tuna.

Suddenly a loud *crash* came out
of the dark, and everyone jumped.
A building that had been damaged
by the quake chose that exact
moment to collapse.

"Wow!" Fatima gasped. "Okay, is everyone all right?"

"Ryan, no!" Anika shouted.

Fatima spun around. She had been facing the fire, so it took a moment for her eyes to adjust to the dark. But by then Ryan was gone.

So was the cat. It had spooked at the noise, and Ryan had run after it. Fatima heard him in the distance, shouting, and caught glimpses of Ryan's torch flashing around.

"Catty, come back!"

"Ryan!" Fatima yelled. But there was no reply.

Suki was crying for her brother,
and Anika looked terrified.

Fatima knew she had to find Ryan.
He might get lost, or run into some
aggressive scavenger.

"Right," she said firmly. She
thought, hard. First thing was to
take care of the girls.

"I have to go and get Ryan. Bear
has to know where you are when
he gets back, and you have to stay
safe – so I want you both to get
into the car, so you can look after
each other and I can concentrate
on finding your brother."

Suki and Anika nodded nervously,
but they climbed in.

Fatima looked around, remembering
something she'd learned at Scouts.
She grabbed an upturned trolley that
was lying nearby and put it on top
of the car.

"This will help Bear know where
you are," she shouted as she worked.
"It will act as a distinct marker in
case he can't find you if I'm still
away."

She paused. "Now keep calm,
right? I won't be long. Hang tight.
Be brave!" And with that she ran
off to find Ryan.

"Right," she muttered to herself
as she ran. "Scavengers or not,
here I come ..."

She knew that there would be hungry animals looking for food. *And they won't all be friendly, Bear had said.* She needed to be able to defend herself.

Fatima remembered seeing a spanner wrench earlier when they had been looking through the cars. It was used for changing tyres. She soon found it again. It was a solid metal bar about thirty centimetres long with a little arm on the end.

She hefted it in one hand and held the torch in the other. Then she followed the direction Ryan had gone.

Her ears picked out the occasional shout of 'cat!' from ahead. Ryan didn't

sound frightened. He just wanted
his furry friend back.

The sounds led Fatima away from
the park. She was on her own now –
in the dark.

"Ryan! Come back here!" She kept
shouting as she hurried towards the
glimpses of his torch in the distance.

Fatima kept her light focused ahead
so that she didn't trip or bump into
anything that could hurt her. She
could see only what was ahead,
the rest was all darkness.

She kept calling Ryan as she went.
The only noise was the sound of her
footsteps echoing back from the walls.

Then she rounded a corner and
the light from her torch lit up Ryan.

"Ryan! Wait right there!" She raced
over towards him. "There you are!"
she breathed with relief.

They were in a small square. Ryan
was stood alone, pointing his torch
up towards a ledge. His face was
heartbroken.

"Cat went up there," he said. Fatima flicked the torch beam up to the ledge but there was no sign of it.

"I expect it's gone back to its friends," she said. "Shall we go back too?"

Ryan pouted.

"Want the cat."

"Well, we've still got some tuna. Maybe the cat will come back for that?"

He looked at her hopefully. She pushed the point again.

"Cats always remember where food is and they can smell it from a long way off."

"Okay," Ryan grumbled.

They made their way back through the dark to the park, guided by the flickering lights from their torches. The girls had got out of the car and were sitting next to the fire again when they got back.

Fatima was about to tell them
off when she saw that Bear had
come back too.

"Hi, there!" he called when he
saw Fatima's torch. "The girls said
you'd gone to get Ryan. All okay?"

He ruffled Ryan's hair, then looked
at Fatima.

"Well done, you," he said with
a sincere smile. "That can't have
been easy, but you did everything
right. Protected the girls, marked
where they were ..."

He glanced at the shopping trolley
on the top of the upside-down vehicle.

125

"And then protected yourself."
This time he looked at the wrench
in her hand. "Smart girl. And brave."

Fatima felt kind of embarrassed
by his praise.

"Well," she said, "I just ..." Her
voice trailed off as she realised
something.

She hadn't been beaten by the dark. A little scared maybe, but definitely less so than before. She had persevered and not given up.

She had been more scared that Ryan might get hurt, than she was by any imaginary monsters.

Wow.

"Did you find anyone?" she asked, to change the subject.

Bear shook his head.

"It was just an automatic security light, battery-powered. Well, we should all turn in. Why not help the kids settle down?"

"Sure," Fatima agreed.

She knelt down to open the
car door. It was stuck. She gave
the handle a big pull and tumbled
backwards as it flew open. Fatima
looked around.

The park had gone. She was no
longer in the city.

"Bear?" she asked. She looked
around. "Ryan? Anika? Suki?"

They were all gone. She was back
at Camp, outside the door to the
shower block.

How had she got back here?

Had she been sleepwalking
and had a really weird dream?

Fatima automatically began to head
back towards her tent, because it
was nippy and there was no sense
in hanging around.

She had picked her way through
the tents and guy ropes, halfway
back, when she realised something
once more.

She wasn't afraid. Well, that
was one thing she *had* brought
back with her from the city. From
now on, imaginary dangers were
just ... well, imaginary.

Fatima looked up. There were no clouds, which meant she could see the stars.

Thousands of them. *Millions.* Pinpricks of light as far as she could see. And there was the Milky Way — a band of light that ran from one side of the sky to the other.

This was the dark, and it was truly beautiful.

10

CLEAN-UP CREW

"Fatima, wake up!"

Her tent-mate Chloe was fully dressed.

"You'll miss breakfast if you sleep any longer!" Chloe said. "Remember we're on clean-up today."

"Oops!"

Fatima sat up quickly and looked around.

It was daytime and the tent was full of light. Sophie had already got up and gone.

"Come on," Chloe said, "I'll see you there!"

She slipped out of the tent, leaving Fatima alone.

Fatima got dressed quickly and went out into the daylight. She reached out wide and let out a big yawn.

After that really weird sleepwalking dream thing last night, Fatima had just sat and stared at the night sky for ages. It had been awesome.

Eventually she had made herself go back inside the tent because she had known she needed some sleep.

And now she needed food, so she hurried after everyone else.

Breakfast was served on trestle tables outside the food tent. It was a busy scene, with a camp full of kids all jostling to get their helpings of cereal, toast, eggs and beans, and everything else that was available. It was always a good start to the day.

But it had to be cleaned up afterwards. Every camper was put into a clean-up team for one meal during Camp, and this morning it was Fatima's turn to help.

The leader in charge gathered them and checked their names on a list.

"And you're Fatima," he said, "so that's everyone except ... Has anyone seen Charlie?"

"Charlie? Charlie!" everyone called.

Charlie was still sitting at a table, with his head over his tablet while his fingers moved against the screen.

He looked up with a sudden guilty expression.

"Oh, sorry ... hang on ..." he said.

His head went back down.

"Charlie," the leader called, "now! Put that away."

Charlie grumpily came over to them. He still held on to the screen, so he hadn't actually put it away.

"Right," the leader said with a smile. "Let's get started. Gather up all the plates and cutlery, uneaten food goes into one of the bags, cutlery goes into this basket here ..."

And so they got to work.

Most of them.

Fatima and Charlie started on opposite sides of one of the long tables, piling everything up.

By the time Fatima was halfway down her side, she realised she was way ahead. Charlie was playing his game again.

"Charlie!" Fatima sounded more impatient than she had meant to.

Charlie scowled. Maybe because they were the same age, he was less polite to her than he had been to the leader.

"Sorry, Mum," he said sarcastically.

Charlie just squished all the plates on his side into a pile, one on top of the other, and then went back to his screen.

Fatima sighed. He wasn't exactly being very kind or helpful – she thought about all the things she'd had to do to keep safe with Bear and the kids in the city. Bear would have reunited the children with their mum by now. Charlie really didn't know how lucky he was here at Camp.

"Come on, Charlie," she said gently. "You're meant to scrape the food off first."

"You do it then," Charlie snapped back angrily, as he went back to his game.

But their conversation had got
the leader's attention. He made
Charlie hand over his tablet, so
that he didn't have a choice about
helping.

"That is so unfair!" he complained
as he started stacking the plates. He
was obviously annoyed as he crashed
them together.

Fatima thought again about her
strange dream last night.

Bear had helped her face up to
the dark, hadn't he? She reckoned
that Bear would be able to find the
right words to help Charlie start
doing his bit and to get positively
involved. But how could she get
Charlie into her dream?

She smiled sadly. *That wasn't going to happen.*

Fatima had built up a big pile of plates to carry over to the kitchen. She thought about asking for Charlie's help but she didn't want to be snapped at again, so she dug her fingers under the pile and lifted them.

The bottom plate was slippery with ketchup and her fingers couldn't get a grip. With horror Fatima felt the whole pile slide through her hands and land on her feet.

"Fatima!" the leader gasped as he hurried over. "Are you okay?"

Fatima stared down. Nothing hurt. Some of the plates had broken but her feet were totally fine.

"Y-yes," she said, surprised. "I'm fine, thanks." But any other words just dried up in her mouth as she realised what she was looking at.

Charlie came running over. His sulk had vanished.

He squinted at her feet.

"Lucky you were wearing those boots," he commented. "It could have really hurt otherwise." He paused. "You okay?"

"Yes. I'm fine," Fatima murmured, still in a daze. "And, uh, thanks, Charlie."

Fatima stared at her feet.

If those plates had fallen onto her rubber clogs, she would definitely have been hurt. The pile had been heavy.

But she was wearing a sturdy pair of boots. She had put them on without thinking when she left the tent in a hurry.

They were the very same walking boots Bear had got for her in the sports store in the mall.

It *hadn't* been a dream.

Fatima got through the rest of the clean-up with her head still spinning. At the end everyone was meant to go off to their activities for the morning. But Fatima sat at one of the tables, deep in thought.

How had she got to the mall? She had left the tent in the dark to use the toilet. She had gone into the bathroom. The lights went out. And then ... what?

Her thoughts were interrupted by electronic squeaks and squawks. She looked round and realised Charlie had also stayed behind. He had his game back and was sitting at the end of the table with his head in another universe.

Sometimes, Fatima thought, *Charlie was perfectly friendly. But he seemed to change the moment he got his game back.*

Fatima got up to go, but then she felt the compass in her pocket.

The compass! Of course! She remembered that had been weird, last night. It had seemed to have five directions, right before she found herself in the clothes store.

Was it the compass that did it?

Maybe the compass could take Charlie to Bear?

Well, nothing ventured, nothing gained.

"Hey, Charlie?" she said. "Want to see something cool?"

"Mm?" He didn't look up, so she put the compass on the table next to him. He picked it up and squinted at it.

"What does it do?" he asked, puzzled.

Fatima smiled.

"Perhaps you'll find out?" she said. "Just consider it a gift."

The End

Bear Grylls got the taste for adventure at a young age from his father, a former Royal Marine. After school, Bear joined the Reserve SAS, then went on to become one of the youngest ever people to climb Mount Everest, just two years after breaking his back in three places during a parachute jump.

Amongst other adventures he has led expeditions to the Arctic and the Antarctic, crossed oceans and set world records in skydiving and paragliding.

Bear is also a bestselling author and the host of television programmes such as *Survival School* and *The Island*.

He has shared his survival skills with people all over the world, and has taken many famous movie stars and sports stars on adventures – and even President Barack Obama!

Bear Grylls is Chief Scout to the UK Scouting Association, encouraging young people to

have great adventures, follow
their dreams and to look after
their friends. Bear is also honorary
Colonel to the Royal Marine
Commandos.

When Bear's not travelling the
world, he lives with his wife and
three sons on a barge in London,
or on an island off the coast of
Wales.

Find out more at
www.beargrylls.com

This brilliant **Bear Grylls Adventure** is set in a reader-friendly font and design, for maximum enjoyment for everyone.

The font we have used is called OpenDyslexic. You can find out more about it here: **www.opendyslexic.org**

Dyslexia affects as many as 1 in 10 people, and often makes reading more difficult. We wanted to make our books as easy to enjoy as possible, so this special font and a design with lots of space helps us do just that.

Not everyone with difficulty reading has dyslexia, and not everyone with dyslexia has the same difficulties. You can find out more about dyslexia on these wonderful websites:

The Dyslexia Association: **dyslexia.uk.net**

British Dyslexia Assocation: **bdadyslexia.org.uk**

Dyslexia Scotland: **www.dyslexiascotland.org.uk**

FOR MORE INFORMATION ON
BEAR GRYLLS, CHECK OUT

beargrylls.com